E
GRI

Griest, Virginia.

In between.

$11.95

69BT00644

DATE			

© THE BAKER & TAYLOR CO.

to my sons
Kim, Barry, Randy and Ken
who taught me to go for it
V.G.

to Jessica Brown
M.W.

In Between

by Virginia Griest

pictures by
Monica Wellington

E. P. Dutton　New York

The grass is here,

the sky is there.

The clouds are

in between.

My cat is here,

a bird is there.

The fence is

in between.

A head is here,

a tail is there.

My dog is in between.

The front door here,

the back door there.

My house is

in between.

A cupboard is here,

the stove is there.

Our table is

in between.

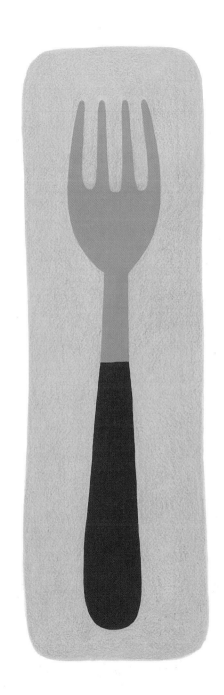

A fork is here,

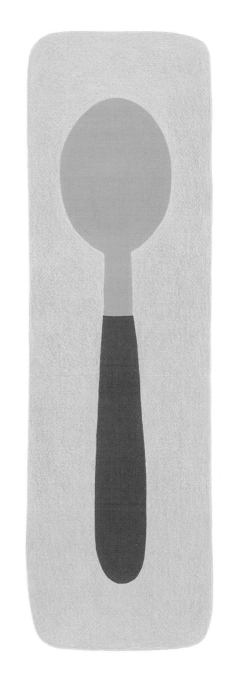

a spoon is there.

My plate is

in between.

Some milk is here,

the cookies there.

My smile is

in between.

My mom is here,

my dad is there.

And I sit in between!

Published in the United States by E. P. Dutton,
a division of Penguin Books USA Inc.

Published simultaneously in Canada by
Fitzhenry & Whiteside Limited, Toronto

Printed in Hong Kong by South China Printing Co.
First Edition   10 9 8 7 6 5 4 3 2 1

Library of Congress Cataloging-in-Publication Data

Griest, Virginia.
    In between/by Virginia Griest; pictures by Monica Wellington.—1st ed.
        p.   cm.
    Summary: Text and pictures illustrate things that are in between,
such as the clouds in between grass and sky, and the child in between
Mom and Dad.
    ISBN 0-525-44521-8
    [1. English language—Adverbs—Fiction.]   I. Wellington,
Monica, ill.   II. Title.   89-30548
PZ7.G88124In   1989   CIP
[E]—dc19   AC